I know you're
"Dad", Kyle ... enjoy the pictures
and stories with the whole family...
Love,
Dad & Mom
Christmas 2003

Every ❧ *Superman* ❧ *Needs A Dad*

By Susan Easton Black

With Illustrations
by Liz Lemon Swindle

MILLENNIAL PRESS
Salt Lake City, Utah

Millennial Press, Inc.
P. O. Box 339
Riverton, Utah 84065

ISBN: #1-930980-94-9

Contents

A look back to a softer society...

Introduction

In the mid-1940s, Americans believed illustrator Norman Rockwell (1894-1978) could render a homey cover of a Thanksgiving dinner on the head of a pin and meet the impossible *Saturday Evening Post* deadline first thing Monday morning. His illustrations, like those of John Falter's (1910-1982) Fourth of July celebrations in Nebraska and Haddon Sundblom's (1899-1976) Coca-Cola Santa Claus, are memories of yesterday.

From great moments in baseball to the flirting maid, artists in the "Golden Age of Illustration" used a paint brush to set the standard for storytelling. They knew descriptive manuscripts, such as those by Sinclair Lewis and Louis Bromfield, begged to be painted. But whether the manuscript was good or bad, magazine publishers expected a colorful, page-turning scene to brighten each story—and they were not disappointed.

"Who would have thought the doctor looked like that," readers said as they turned pages of the *Post, Cosmopolitan* and *Good Housekeeping*. But when the Post replaced the paint brush with photography, such comments stopped and illustration scurried out the back door.

"The *Saturday Evening Post* struck a death knell to our trade," illustrators cried. No one argues that the "Golden Age of Illustration" ended, but illustration did not become a lost art. Award-winning artist Liz Lemon Swindle, knowing that illustration has been her stepping-stone to the gallery, celebrates the pictorial storytellers of the past in *Every Superman Needs a Dad*. With writer Susan Easton Black, she looks back to a softer society—a time when a good laugh was fun, kindness was expected and romance started with holding hands. Together Black and Swindle look to an era when the sentimental story had a moral ending and living happily ever after was believable. They hope that you also see in *Every Superman Needs a Dad* a time when fiction was so realistic you knew the writer had met your Uncle Harry.

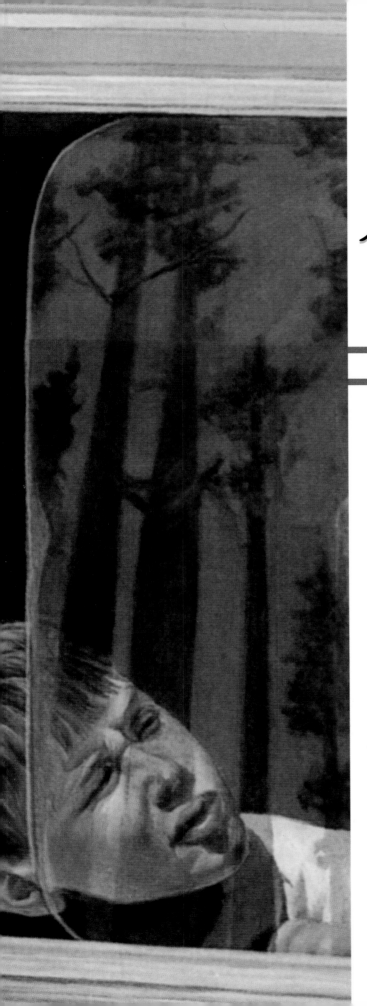

Aunt Jane & the Cowboy

Although my aunt has sworn vengeance if I tell the truth about how she fell in love with Slim Perkins, I can't keep quiet any longer. To do so wrecks my insides. "Ulcers forming on your intestines," said the doctor. "Need to let out what's bothering you, son," he said. So on my doctor's advice, and your promise to protect me from Aunt Jane, here goes.

"I don't want Aunt Jane to go on our camping trip!" I firmly stated to my dad. His sister Jane had just been left at the altar for the third time, and Dad thought the right cure for a rejected bride was a camping trip with our family.

"Jane is a pain on a camping trip," I cried. Last year I asked her, 'Why did the chicken cross the road?' Instead of the simple answer, 'To get to the other side,' Her response was to ask, 'How wide was the road and how long was the stride of the chicken?' By the time she waxed eloquent about a chicken moving slower on an asphalt road than a cement highway, I didn't care if she answered the question or not.

"Three years in a row on our family campout is too much," I said to Dad.

"You'll like it this time," Dad said as he pushed aside newspapers on the kitchen table and spread out a brochure featuring a dude ranch in Antimony, Utah. Photographs of riding horses, rustling cattle and roping steers at Antimony soon replaced my reluctance to include Aunt Jane for the third time. In fact, my brothers and I became so excited about a dude ranch adventure that we marked off each day on the calendar in anticipation.

The day our adventure began, Aunt Jane arrived at our house still moping about the man that got away. While my mother consoled her, we loaded the tent, sleeping bags, wood and camping gear into the trailer.

"Let's go," said Dad as he started the motor. As I ran toward the trailer Dad shouted, "Did you get the gasoline for our campfires like I asked you?"

"No," I replied. "But I'll get it right now." I hurried to the garage and found the gasoline in the large red container. Knowing that we needed only a small quantity, I searched the garage for a discarded bottle. After filling an old Gatorade bottle with gasoline, I returned to the trailer announcing, "All set."

As Dad drove toward Antimony, Mother did needle work to pass the time. My brothers and I played cards and Jane, the unrestrained school teacher, interjected into our card game such comments as, "Billy has fifty-two points. What five cards equal fifty-two?"

"She is a total pain," I said to myself, trying to make the photographic images of horses and steers crowd out her words.

Near dusk we pulled into the parking lot of the celebrated dude ranch. "It surely is hot," said my brother Tim as he opened the trailer door.

Correcting his grammar Aunt Jane said, "'Surely' is not needed in the sentence. Simply, 'It is hot' will do."

Just as Tim was whispering unkind words about Jane, a tall cowboy from across the pasture yelled, "Howdy folks."

In the spirit of the dude ranch, I hollered back, "Howdy partner."

As Cowboy Slim Perkins approached the trailer he said, "It's so darn hot, I've got cotton mouth."

My inquisitive aunt asked, "What's cotton mouth?"

Without explaining, Slim grabbed her hand and spit on it. He then pointed to the white, nearly foaming spittle and said, "That's cotton mouth, ma'am."

"Why, I never," said my aunt as she rushed inside the trailer in search of a washcloth and soap. She found more than soap and a cloth that day; she found the Gatorade bottle. All I remember hearing from inside the trailer was a scream and a series of belches. Before I could rush inside to see what was the matter, Aunt Jane stumbled out of the trailer holding the Gatorade bottle in her hand.

"She drunk gas," I said.

Aunt Jane was too busy belching to correct my English this time.

"How in the Sam blazes did gasoline get in a Gatorade bottle?" asked Dad.

Before I could explain, Slim picked up Aunt Jane and ran with her belching and screaming to the horse trough. He dropped her, shoes and all, smack dab in the middle of the trough and dunked her head under the water. She tried to hit him each time he shoved her head under the dirty water.

"Slow down missy," said Slim. "You'll be okay in a minute."

It took her a lot longer than a minute to feel better. In fact, we had her sit down wind from our campfire so that her belching wouldn't set the forest ablaze.

Slim tried to comfort her by singing his original cowboy songs. I was partial to "I am Ugly as Sin and Ought to be Shot," but Aunt Jane didn't seem to enjoy his guitar playing or lyrics. I had the feeling that she was more upset about the gasoline and being dunked in the horse trough than being jilted at the altar.

By the next morning everything seemed better, but it was hard to tell because Aunt Jane hadn't emerged from her tent. By the time we finished breakfast Slim had arrived to escort us to the lake for "Ol' Fashion Cowboy Fun."

"Are you coming?" Dad hollered toward Jane's tent.

To my surprise Aunt Jane stepped from the tent wearing a glittering cowgirl outfit.

"Got your bathing suit on?" Dad asked. "It's going to be a great day at the lake."

"Sure," said Jane as she joined the family and Slim. After an hour of hiking, Jane was the first to see the lake. She spoke poetically of crystal water and swishing cattails, but sensing that no one was listening, she ripped off her cowgirl shirt and pants and shouted, "Last one to the lake is a rotten egg."

Although Jane ran, none of us moved or spoke. We were too shocked. Slim broke the silence by asking, "What is that white stuff your aunt has hanging from her bathing suit?"

None of us could explain the white netting. It wasn't until my mother said, "Oh my goodness! Jane has her bathing suit on inside out," that we knew.

When Jane reached the lake, she turned around and shouted, "I won!" Seeing the rest of us staring at her and not having joined in the race she asked, "What's wrong?"

It was Cowboy Slim who told her.

I never saw anyone hit the dirt faster or slither into the water quicker than Aunt Jane.

If the rodeo hadn't been more defining to the relationship of Slim and Aunt Jane than the wrong-sided bathing suit, I would tell you more about the lake adventures. But that afternoon the dude ranch was sponsoring a rodeo for amateurs. Catching the spirit of the ranch, Aunt Jane and I decided to enter the steer-roping contest. It was agreed that I would tie the front legs of the steer and Jane the hind legs.

As we entered the make-shift arena, my aunt said, "We'll just tie up that steer and toss him to the ground in record time." To my complete satisfaction, I roped the front legs of that animal on my first try. But no matter what Jane did, she could not rope the hind legs.

"Hold the steer still," Dad yelled from the sidelines.

I hollered, "Aunt Jane, pull on the tail," thinking that such action would startle the steer so that Jane could lasso the hooves.

Jane followed my advice. She lifted the tail and pulled with all her might. I don't think Aunt Jane knew much about cow pies before that day. But at the rodeo in Antimony, she became an authority. She tried to stop the output by pulling the tail downward and even holding it in place. It might have worked if she had not lost her footing.

It was Slim who ran to her rescue. He scooped her into his arms and ran with her to the horse trough. Needless to say, we didn't win the steer-roping contest, but I did pick flowers for my aunt as a consolation prize.

It wasn't until Slim Perkins was walking toward our campground that I handed the flowers to her. "These flowers are for you," I said, pointing toward Slim to let her know that he was approaching. She thought I was pointing to Slim because he had picked the flowers for her. Before I could explain, she ran to the cowboy and kissed him on the cheek. Slim looked puzzled.

"That's no way to kiss a cowboy, ma'am," he said.

What happened next was not a pretty sight. He lifted Aunt Jane into his arms and kissed her good.

The vacation ended but Aunt Jane stayed in Antimony. Three months later she and cowboy Slim were married. Mom was the bridesmaid and Dad the best man. I was the ring bearer, and not the flower girl like my brothers say.

Uncle Slim and Aunt Jane live in Antimony and may never know I wrote this story. What they do know is that they both get cotton mouth and live happily ever after—or at least reasonably so. As for me, my stomach feels better already.

This is My Neighborhood

As Caucasian families fled from urban upheaval in Los Angeles to the suburbs in the 1990s, the formerly all-white neighborhoods took on a darker complexion, and property values plummeted. Noting the "white flight" and spiraling market trend, my blonde hair, blue-eyed father announced to our family, "I know the perfect place to live—it's on the edge of Watts. Just a five-minute walk to St. Mary's Hospital."

Aunt Margaret was incensed with his depiction of the "perfect neighborhood." "People are afraid to walk the streets after dark in that neighborhood. Women report being threatened and knocked to the ground," she said. Her talk of vandalism, high crime and growing drug problems fell on deaf ears. Even her comment, "This neighborhood will never welcome a skinny 5'4" male nurse" did not change my dad's decision.

The day we began unloading boxes into our new home in Watts caused nearby neighbors to whisper and stare in disbelief. The only whites for blocks were widows, lacking funds to leave the neighborhood, and single-parent families, who couldn't afford housing elsewhere. Then there was our family—three American-looking Swedes.

I swear my father was color-blind that day and in the days that followed. He never spoke of our neighborhood as a microcosm of ethnicity—Blacks, Latinos, Samoans, Tongans, Vietnamese, Cambodians, and Laotians—or that we were the minority in the "tossed salad" of Los Angeles. He only spoke of newfound friends on his five-minute walk to the hospital.

One day Mom and I followed him on his walk. We observed him bandage the bruised knee of a little boy, nail a loose fence post back in place and share a joke with an elderly widow: "Different strokes for different folks said the farmer as he kissed the cow." The next day we followed him again only to discover that the morning before was typical.

On Saturday mornings Dad took me to the sandlot to watch neighbors play football. We clapped and cheered as if we were seated on the sideline at the Superbowl. Saturday afternoon Dad made house calls to repair leaky roofs, fix small appliances and share a friendly hello.

It was my playmate Mina, the Tongan girl next door, who first called my dad "Doc." Dad assured her that he was only a nurse. But to Mina and those residing along his walking route, he was "Doc." He struggled with the nickname for he had taken the qualifying medical exams twice and failed. "Third time's a charm," he assured us.

The third time occurred on the day in 1992 when the accused assailants of Rodney King were found not guilty. The verdict shocked our neighbors as all had seen King's video-taped beating by police officers on television. Angered with the verdict, minority youth took to the streets rioting against oppression, both real and imagined. It seemed that any hope of fairness to minorities was replaced with fists, guns, fire and destruction.

Looting scenes captured by television crews riveted my family and me. Watching shopping malls, grocery stores and apartment houses being destroyed caused us great unrest. The unrest was accentuated when police, over loud speakers in their patrol cars, advised: "White people: leave your homes immediately. Shelters have been set up outside the Watts area to provide you safety."

We were stunned. Was the advice meant for us? I actually think it was the first time my father saw skin tone as he looked at Mom and me. Realizing the danger, he insisted that my mother and I take a few things from our home and go quickly to the shelter. My mother ran through the house gathering legal papers, valuable dishes and heirlooms. I ran into my bedroom and gathered all my dolls and teddy bears. Each of my treasured possessions were hurled into the trunk of our old Chevy.

Through this gathering process, my father sat quietly in the rocking chair in the living room. "You had better move it!" I heard my mother say.

"I am not leaving—not just yet," said Dad.

My bewildered mother had precious little time to convince him. My mother and I sped through the streets faster than I thought the Chevy could go. We found the shelter crowded with "whites" expressing fear. Although my mother was also afraid she insisted that my daily routine not be disrupted.

"It's nap time for you, Hannah," she stated. I lined up my dolls and teddy bears on the bed that was provided, but I couldn't close my eyes. I cuddled my favorite doll in my arms and wished that my dad could see the bears and dolls again. I wondered when he would come to the shelter.

While these thoughts stole sleep from my eyes, my dad was cleaning up the mess in our house created by our hurried departure. Afterward he climbed up a ladder to inspect the damage caused by a fire bomb to the roof. He discovered that a fire-laden bomb had burned a hole through the shingles. He also found that the nearby market had been set ablaze. After surveying the growing dilemma, he descended the ladder.

Standing in our front yard was Mina. "Can Hannah come out to play dolls?" Mina asked.

"I'm sorry Mina. Hannah and her mother have gone to the shelter," he replied.

"Are you going, too?" inquired Mina.

"No," said Dad.

"Father, Doc's not leaving the neighborhood," she yelled as she ran to her house.

Mina's father burst out his front door and spoke sharply to my dad. "You must go! It is too dangerous for you to stay," he said.

Although Dad listened, he would not budge. "Thanks for caring. I love being your neighbor and I will be your neighbor tonight. This is my neighborhood, too."

Mina, who had been tugging at her father's pant leg, exclaimed, "We have to help Doc!" As Mina ran to nearby neighbors asking for help, her mother telephoned friends and her father walked the five-minute route to the hospital to spread the word.

"Doc won't leave the neighborhood," he shouted.

An hour later Dad heard Mina calling him from our front yard. "Doc, friends of yours are here to help," she said. As my dad looked out the window, he saw over a hundred neighbors ranging in age from Mina to an elderly widow.

As he came out the front door he said, "You are placing yourselves in danger. I can't ask you to risk your lives for me."

"You aren't asking," said Mina's father. "I asked and they all came. Now keep that white face of yours inside. We have a job to do!"

A while later about sixty looters broke into the corner liquor store. Notified of the break-in, police drove to the scene demanding that looters leave the premises. They left the store but moved as a group toward our house shouting, "Rodney King—let us in."

"No!" was the unified shout from neighbors standing in our yard.

"Move aside brother; this isn't your house," intoxicated youth yelled.

"You don't act like my brother," said Mina's father. "Doc is our brother! Now leave him alone or you will face us. You don't want a Tongan mad . . . or do you?"

For two nights drunken looters returned to our house chanting, "Rodney King—let us in," and for two nights they were repelled by our neighbors.

"Why jeopardize your life for him?" a reporter from CNN asked Mina's father.

"Doc's my friend," was his reply.

"Why did your ethnically diverse neighbors risk their lives for you?" the same reporter asked Dad.

"They love me," he said simply.

Not everyone is able to remove the blinders of prejudice to see the true value of another, but a neighborhood in east Los Angeles did in 1992. Because of their bravery, Dad was able to come to the shelter later and see my dolls and teddy bears lined up on the bed. He liked them and hugged each one. But I think he liked seeing me best of all because he hugged me the most.

About a month after the riots, Dad received a letter assuring him that the "third time was the charm." He had passed the qualifying medical examination and received an appointment to enter the University of Southern California Medical School.

"That's great," he said. And with the same enthusiasm continued, "I won't have to leave my neighborhood!"

Upon graduation from medical school, Dad accepted a physician's position at St. Mary's Hospital. We still live in the same house and Dad walks to work along his five-minute route just in case any of his neighbors need assistance.

A Plate of Cookies

"I can't believe it!" said Stella. "What?" asked her bewildered husband. "Your napkin is still on the table and you are eating!" Rather than hang his head or murmur, as was his later habit, George simply replied, "I was hoping that such comments could wait until after the honeymoon."

They didn't wait for the honeymoon to end or in the days that followed. A critical glance, a wagging tongue and sharp words were hurled at George as if he had a thick veneer. He didn't. With a pretense of regret, he left Stella.

We could not. Stella was our next-door neighbor, and as much as my brothers and I wanted to move—even offering allowances and proceeds from lemonade sales to facilitate the move—all offers were refused.

"Stella is our neighbor whether you like it or not," my father stated. His firm stance nearly ruined my childhood. His displeasure over my actions and warnings not to irritate Stella became the norm. And what made matters worse was that we lived on one side of the duplex and she on the other.

Day after day she sat near her window with needle in hand in the pretense of doing stitchery, but my brothers and I knew better. She looked out the window with every stitch hoping to see our misdeeds and then tattle on us.

Stella was not nice. Even my saintly mother said so. No one liked her—not her former husband and surely not me. But as with every good story there developed an unusual twist. In the life of Stella and me it began when my mother said, "Each child in this family will do something nice for Stella."

My oldest brother Brian agreed. "I will give her flowers," he said. As my mother beamed with approval, he added, "I will pick a bouquet from her window box just for her."

My brother Todd said, "I will shovel her snowy walks." Peals of laughter were heard that day as the August sunlight streamed through our window. Joining the merriment I added, "I will bake her cookies." Failing to have a witty retort my brothers grimaced at my lack of creativity. But when my mother left the room I assured them I would mix castor oil and our special brand of hot sauce in the cookie dough. They approved of my plan.

Brian never did pick the flowers, but I baked the cookies. To my chagrin Mother watched carefully as each ingredient was added to the cookie mixture. I tried to distract her by saying, "I don't need your help," but she was not diverted. By the time the cookies were baking in the oven any hope of Stella's wrenching stomach ache were gone.

"Can I have some cookies?" Todd asked Mother as he came running into the kitchen.

"Only a few," she replied. "Judy has made the cookies for Stella." Todd didn't laugh out loud, but he did give me the "Way to go!" smile. When Mother offered him hot cookies and milk, he feigned that he wasn't hungry anymore. I never explained to him that the castor oil and hot sauce had to wait for another day.

With a plate of cookies in my hands, I timidly approached Stella's side of the duplex.

"What do you want?" she asked.

With hesitation I replied, "I have brought you a plate of cookies." As she took them from me, I saw a fleeting smile.

As the days passed, Stella sat near her window and stitched on her needle work. I liked her stitchery and stared in the window as she sewed. When she saw me I waved and once I thought she nodded in my direction.

Then came November and with it a change of weather and a new development in our duplex. It began as my mother awoke to find a few inches of snow covering the ground. She awakened Todd. "It snowed through the night," she announced.

Although sleepy-eyed, Todd couldn't believe his misfortune. "I haven't waxed my skis. How could it have snowed already?" he asked. Mother told him not to worry about waxing skis, building snowmen or throwing snowballs. "Stella needs her walk shoveled," she said.

"You remembered?" Todd moaned.

Yes, she had remembered his merriment when he visualized shoveling Stella's snowy walks in August. Todd grabbed his coat, hat and gloves and meandered out the front door. Within a few moments he entered the house and announced, "I can't shovel her walkway!" Mother assured him that she was not making a casual request. "I can't shovel her walks. Stella has already shoveled them," Todd stated.

Knowing the neighbor's age and physical infirmities my mother expressed her embarrassment over the situation. "I should have awakened you earlier. Stella shouldn't have to shovel the walks," she said.

Todd pointed toward the window. As Mother looked through the frosty window pane she was surprised to see Stella shoveling our walkway. "What's she doing?" Mother asked as she dashed out the front door.

"She's shoveling our walks," Todd said as he followed her. My mother hugged Stella and Todd patted her shoulder. Stella began to cry and I couldn't help myself—I started to like her. I ran outside and said, "Thank you."

The days of living next door to an unfriendly old woman melted away as I saw my neighbor—for the first time—as nice. Giving cookies and shoveling snow normally don't have much in common, but to Stella and me they became one and the same.

My neighbor still sits by the window and embroiders. Although she stitches on quilts, hand towels and pillow cases, my favorite stitchery is the one she made for me. It depicts a little girl with cookies and an old woman with a shovel, and both are happy.

Every *Superman* Needs a Dad

Burned flags and lives of patriots cut short are too often today's remembrances of the Vietnam War. But for me, as a young boy growing up in the 1960s, the war wasn't about destruction—it was about my dad.

My dad was stationed at Fort Riley, Kansas. He was a combat pilot in the Air Force. He was very patriotic and sympathetic to the war and, wanting to be just like him, so was I. My room was decorated in red, white and blue. From the bedspread to the posters on the wall everything said, "American made" and "the American way." Model rockets and airplanes that my dad and I had built together were my prized possessions—that was until he was called to active duty.

As much as I loved my country, I didn't want my dad flying over war zones in Vietnam. But my wants were not to be realized. "Timmy, you are the man of the house now. Take care of your mother and your baby sister, Dorothy," he said.

"I don't want to be the man of the house," I snapped as he reached for a package hidden between the slip covers of the couch.

"Who could this be for?" he mused. "On the card it reads, 'This is for the man of the house.' The name on the card is Timmy Hill. It must be for you."

I tore open the wrapping paper and discarded the bright ribbon in hopes of finding a model airplane. I was disappointed to see a Superman cape.

"You will be able to leap tall buildings in a single bound and even attract Lois Lane wearing this cape," Dad quipped as he tied the Superman cape around my neck. He then bid me farewell.

It seems odd for a grown man to admit that wearing the Superman cape made any difference—but that's just what happened. I felt more confident. I began to spread peanut butter on my own sandwiches without asking Mom for help. I wore that cape everywhere—in the sandbox, the bathtub and at church.

"Isn't Timmy cute in the cape?" adults remarked. Friends were less kind. "How's Lois?" they asked. "Are you a bird, a plane or could you be Superman?" Strangers shouted, "Show me how to leap a tall building and fly faster than a speeding bullet."

As the days of my dad's absence grew into months, I wore the cape less often. However I always kept it near my pillow, next to GI Joe and the airplane models. When the house was still and my thoughts wandered to whether my dad would come home, I clutched the cape for assurance that all was well.

The day my dad returned to Fort Riley was a day I'll never forget—it was a hero's welcome. The military band played and the air force officers wore their finest uniforms. I proudly wore my Superman cape. During the awards ceremony, Dad insisted that I sit on his lap. When his name was called to step forward and receive a medal for bravery, he insisted that I come forward, too. He had the commanding officer pin the medal on my cape.

"My son Timmy is the real hero," Dad announced over the microphone. "He was the man of the house while I was gone."

Years have passed since that awards ceremony. And like my dad I became a fighter pilot. I have flown many missions that have taken me to military bases throughout the United States and abroad. In my absence, my family raises an American flag on a flagpole in our front yard. Below the flag is my Superman cape for extra courage. Neighbors and curious passersby often ask my wife, "Why the cape?" She shares with them the story of my dad, and so it has been for years.

But on September 11, 2001, everything changed. That day I raised the flag and the Superman cape at half-mast in our front yard. With the Twin Towers in New York City destroyed, I knew it would not be long until I would be called into a war zone—like my dad had been decades before.

Within a few weeks, I received notice that I would be transporting soldiers to Afghanistan for an extended stay. News of the assignment was difficult for my wife and children. I knew that they needed extra emotional support. Wanting them to have the best, I visited my bedridden dad.

"I need you to take care of Mother, sister Dorothy and my own family," I said.

Dad lamented, "I am too old and too sick. I can't do it." He then gave a detailed explanation of his afflictions.

I listened attentively to his rationale before handing him a wrapped package tied with a red, white and blue ribbon. He brightened as his gnarled hands removed the wrapping paper to reveal its hidden contents. Inside the package was a tattered Superman cape and a note that read, "You can leap tall buildings in a single bound and even attract Lois Lane wearing this." I tied the Superman cape around Dad's neck and bid him farewell.

I left for a war zone. My dad, attired in the Superman cape, arose from his sick bed with the same courage he inspired in a younger hero many years before. He showed me once again that every superman needs a dad.

Grandpa Joe & His Marbles

Some grandfathers play catch, horse shoes and golf—not Grandpa Joe. He plays marbles. Once I tried to make him choose between playing softball or basketball, but he wouldn't choose. Marbles is his game—his only game. If I want to have fun with Grandpa I play marbles, too. He draws a perfect circle in the dirt. We each take marbles from our sack, one-by-one, and the game begins. Every time we play, I lose . . . until today.

My victory this afternoon was greater than the ribbons I have won at the county fair for my pig, Chester. I beat Grandpa at his own game. After winning I didn't receive a pat on the back or the congratulatory, "Way to go!" comment. Instead he handed me his shooter and told me this story.

"I grew up during the Great Depression—a time in the United States when families had everything money could not buy. My parents did not accept subsistence living and moved our family from coast to coast and all points in-between chasing the elusive American Dream—big house, fancy car and a stunning mink coat. After years of seeking greener pastures in the next community, our family settled in Payson, Iowa. Payson is not a booming metropolis today and certainly was not in the 1930s.

"Father made a token down payment on a small two-bedroom house and five acres of farmland in Payson. Mother agreed that she would care for the house, the cooking and the laundry, while the men of the family did the outside work. My brother George was responsible for the livestock, Fred the orchard, and me the fields.

Seeing all the outside work delegated, I asked my father, "What will you be doing?" "Supervisor," he said.

Days rolled into months, and months to years and Dad supervised from his vantage point on the porch. I didn't think we needed as much supervising as an additional hand, but Father didn't see it that way.

"Although my brothers and I worked hard, there were always more needs and wants than money in our family. Random odd jobs, like shining shoes and running errands, added precious little to our family coffers. With work seeming to never end, I didn't play basketball or softball, and I don't know any friends who enjoyed such luxuries in Payson. All of us worked, but all of us did play marbles.

"I never viewed marbles as a game of chance—it was imperative to win. Victory meant that my brothers would help me in the fields. I gave one marble for each row they harvested.

"By harvest season of 1935, I had won so many marbles from lesser opponents that my marbles filled two large sacks. One sack contained chipped marbles and the other shiny, polished ones. Among the polished marbles was my favorite—the shooter.

"One afternoon as I lay on my bed counting marbles, Mother asked me to come to the parlor. Dutifully I responded, leaving my prized possessions. Seated on the couch in our parlor was Mrs. Johnson and her son Sam, my best friend. I saw Mrs. Johnson wiping her eyes with a handkerchief and Sam trying to fight back tears.

"'What's up?' I asked.

"'Sam's father got his leg caught in the thresher this afternoon and has been taken to the hospital. He may need to have his leg amputated,' explained my mother. Almost in the same breath she asked, 'Can you take Sam around back and play marbles with him? I want to talk to Mildred alone.'

"'Sure,' I said. Sam gratefully left the parlor and followed me. We gathered my treasures from off the bed and scurried out back. I drew a perfect circle in the dirt and offered Sam the use of my chipped marbles. I knew that he was upset about his father, but this was our game and Sam was good. I needed the edge, the shiny spheres—harvest was next week.

"Again and again, to my complete satisfaction, I was victorious over Sam. One game I let him use my shooter. But even with the shooter he was no match for me. I couldn't lose that day.

"'Can I take home your bag of chipped marbles to practice my game?' Sam asked. 'I'll return them tomorrow.'

"'No!' was my quick retort. 'I can't chance one marble being lost. Harvest is next week.'

"No sooner had I uttered these words than the telephone rang. 'Yes, Mrs. Johnson is here. I will get her for you,' I heard my mother say. Sam and I ran to the parlor just as his mother reached for the telephone. The only words I remember were 'hospital,' 'complication' and 'hurry.' Mother, Mrs. Johnson and Sam ran to the car. Sam was crying now.

"I went to the backyard to pick up my marbles. But the routine of picking them up one-by-one, which had brought me joy day after day, lost its significance that afternoon. I turned to look toward the car and saw Sam just as he was opening the car door.

"'Wait!' I yelled. I picked up my sack, the one with the shiny marbles and my favorite shooter, and ran toward Sam. Sam stood outside the car until I reached him. 'These are for you!' I said, thrusting my sack filled with shiny marbles into his hands.

"It's hard to say what happened that day. I gave away my most precious possessions to my best friend. Fred didn't understand. 'You will have to do all the harvesting yourself this year,' he said.

"I knew it, but it didn't matter then or in the days of toil that followed. Something within me was born that day, the day Sam's father died. I learned that to give is to receive and to receive is to possess joy. You see, Sam is still my best friend. We get together once a week and play marbles. That old shooter has bounced back and forth between us for decades."

Just as my grandfather was ending his story and reaching for his handkerchief to wipe his eyes he said, "Jared, the shooter is yours. You won it fair and square. May the shooter teach you the lessons of life it has taught me."

Without saying another word he stood up and began to walk to his home. That day I think he walked a little taller. A legacy—a shooter—had passed to his grandson.

Frills & Football

My dad is a burley, unkempt man. The only things he takes pride in are his rusty truck and hunting dog. Mom says Dad was quite the ladies man in high school—all-state football and popular, too. Trophies and photographs of cheerleaders waving from dated Corvettes suggest that possibility, but to me Dad is a bore.

His boasts of catching the biggest fish west of the Mississippi and shooting a charging bull square in the eye with a sling-shot and one small stone are just too much for me.

I told Mom that he exaggerates, but she doesn't seem to care. She doesn't realize that I like to hear the classic stories of Cinderella, Sleeping Beauty and Snow White. I don't like listening to Dad's daring adventures on lion safaris in Africa, moose hunts in Sweden, or elephant escapades in India.

If you think it couldn't be worse, it is. Saturday morning he insists on watching football reruns on television. On Sunday, Dad speaks of nothing but NFL football. His idea of a great Sunday is the remote control in one hand and a can of pop in the other. That's not my idea of even a good Sunday.

I want to like my dad and think he is fun, but I can't. My mom likes him. I can't figure it out. She talks non-stop of being a homecoming queen and of the latest fashions. Although Dad nods his head occasionally as she recalls her unparalleled beauty, he doesn't really listen. He's cleaning his shotgun and thinking of last night's card game.

You may think that I haven't tried to establish a "father-daughter" relationship. I have. One day I asked, "Do you want to play?"

"Sure," he said as he reached for his football.

"I don't want to play football—I want to play dress-up," I explained.

Dad refused to play dress-up. "It smacks of frills," he said. He hadn't forgotten the day I painted his toenail red to match his flannel shirt. I never heard such hollering from a grown man in my life when he saw that red toe. You'd have thought Grandma had been seen driving his truck.

My dad and I have just one thing we both like—his hunting dog, Butch. At night and on the weekends, Butch is his dog. But when Dad goes to work at Pierson's Grocery Store, Butch and I play dress-up. Of course neither of us tell Dad. It is our little secret. No telling what he would say. Butch makes a beautiful bride but a better dancer. When I hold a dog biscuit up high in the air, he dances on his hind legs just like Ginger Rogers.

Lately I have been dressing him in my ballerina leotard. The pink tights fit, but he complains that the leotard is too snug. I thought I was making progress with Butch and the leotard until today. It all happened so fast that it's hard to explain. I was sitting on my bed playing with my dolls when I heard Dad's truck door slam. I listened as he walked up the sidewalk and stepped on the front porch. As he was opening the door he said, "Terry tried to put 7-up in the Coca-Cola ice box this . . . " and then he stopped in mid-sentence.

"What in the Sam Hill?" he yelled. "Helen!"

Dad never called Mom Helen, unless he was mad. My mother, wiping her hands on her apron, quickly came to the porch. She didn't have time to say, "What?" for Dad was in no mood for "What?"

"I wanted Sam and you gave me Samantha. Then came Jacqueline instead of Jack. I wanted George and you gave me Georgia and then Tomasina, not Tom. I have tried to maintain my manhood in a house full of females, but Butch in pink tights is too much!" exclaimed Dad.

Those were his last words as he stepped off the porch, marched down the side walk, got into his truck and sped away. Butch whined, Mom went to the bedroom and shut the door, and I left my dolls lined up on the bed to go to the front porch to think. I had to make things right, but how? I thought of baking a cake, ironing a shirt and shining trophies, but none seemed to be just the right answer.

It wasn't until I walked inside the house and saw Dad's football that I knew what I had to do. I picked up the football, put it under my arm and walked down the road to Pierson's Grocery Store. I hadn't anticipated that the boys from school would still be standing by the Coca-Cola cooler. I tried to sneak past them, but it didn't work.

"Samantha, is that you carrying a football?" Terry asked.

"Are you going to be a football star like your Dad?" Billy mocked.

They burst out laughing, but I ignored their remarks and walked right past them and up to the front door of the grocery store. I knocked loud, but Dad must not have heard me. I knocked again, but he must have thought it was one of the boys and didn't come out.

When I knocked on the window, he looked up and saw me but didn't even say "Hello."

With a loud, gruff voice I hollered, "Do you want to play?"

"No," said Dad without looking up. "I don't want to play dress-up."

"I didn't come to play dress-up," I said. "I came to play football. I hear that there's a man in this grocery store who set school records that still aren't broken."

Dad looked up from behind the grocery counter and saw that I was holding his football.

"Can you throw that thing?" he asked.

I gave it such a hard toss that even the boys at the Coca-Cola cooler whistled.

"You throw like a quarterback," Billy said. "What an arm."

"I'll meet you out back," Dad said as he moved away from the counter.

We played until dusk, my dad and me. He gave me tips on punting, running and passing. Although he thought I had promise he said, "You need to practice every night if you are going to make the high school team in ten years."

"I have something I want to say to you, too," I said. "I'm sorry that I dressed Butch in my ballerina leotard and pink tights."

"No harm done," Dad said. "Can you forgive me for not knowing how to be a father to a girl?"

"Sure," I said.

"Would you like to play dress-up?" he asked.

"No. I think I have played dress-up one too many times today. But tomorrow night after football practice, do you want to have a tea party?" I asked.

"Sure," said Dad.

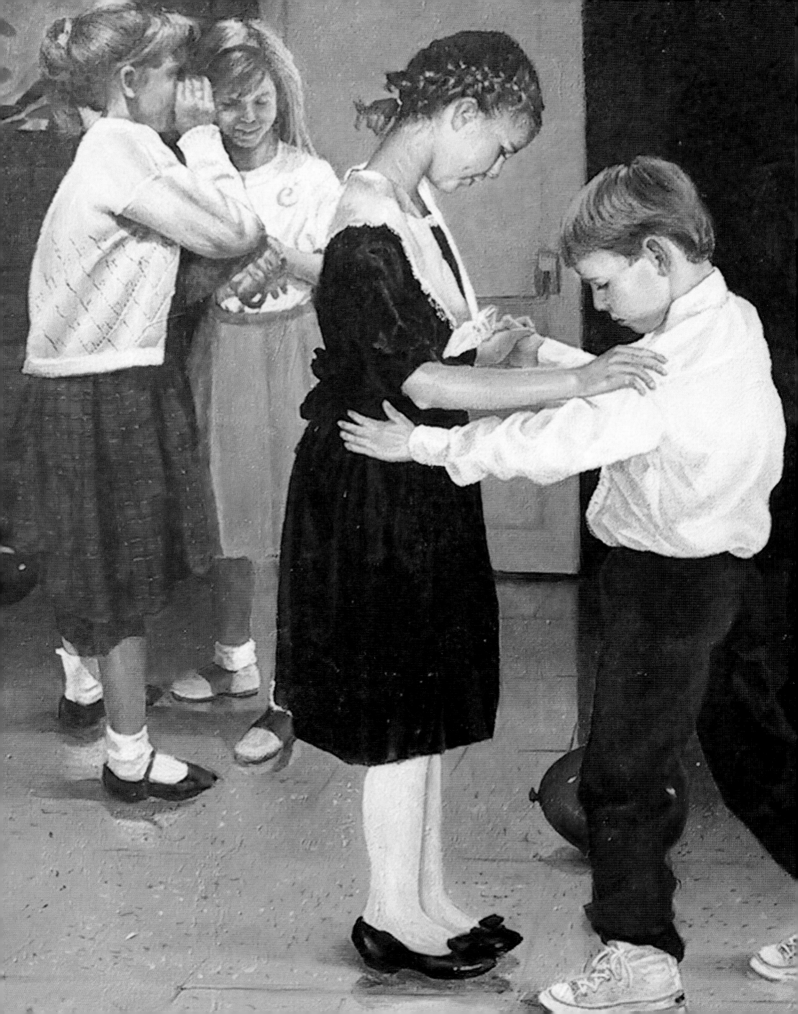

Nothing Can Be That Bad

"**I**'m running away from home and that's final!" Susie said.

"You can't leave," cried Joanna. "Nothing can be that bad."

"Tell us what happened at the dance," Wendy said. "Maybe we can fix it."

"It's too awful. It's the worst thing you can imagine," sobbed Susie. "If I tell you—can you keep a secret?"

"Cross my heart and hope to die," said Joanna and Wendy in unison.

"Do you know Danny Lilly?" Susie asked.

"Danny Lilly is the closest thing I've got to the right answer," said Joanna. "Spelling, multiplication tables and state capitols—he knows it all."

"Miss Gardner says 'Danny is a genius,'" said Wendy. "But to me he's the ultimate nerd. I wouldn't be caught dead even looking at him."

Joanna added, "At the last little league game I saw Danny run to second base from third instead of running to home plate when Daren slammed the baseball down the third base line."

Susie said, "I know all of that, but someday Albert Einstein will be asked, 'How does it feel to be the smartest man born in the twentieth century?' And his response will be, 'I don't know—ask Danny Lilly.'"

Joanna glanced at Wendy and then at Susie. "What are you trying to tell us?" she asked.

"Last week when Miss Gardner announced that Danny scored a hundred percent on his reading test, I was too busy putting polish on my fingernails to notice him. When she said that he scored the highest on the statewide mathematics test, I just kept brushing my hair and admiring my reflection in the window pane. Then I heard Danny ask Miss Gardner, 'Can I sit behind Susie? I'm having trouble seeing the chalkboard.' Because he's the teacher's pet, she didn't question his motives.

"He took the chair behind mine and tapped me on the shoulder, but I didn't turn around. It wasn't until he colored the ends of my hair with permanent markers that I spoke.

"You're a nerd, Danny," I said.

"Will you be my girl friend?" he asked.

"I didn't answer him. The next day I brought a signed note from home requesting a chair on the other side of the classroom.

"Yesterday Danny chased me into the girl's bathroom. I stayed there until after the bell rang and was sure that he had gone. Upon returning to the classroom, I sent him a message that read: 'Leave me alone.'

"I confided in Jim Grow my problem with Danny. He assured me that he would help. By the afternoon 'Kick me!' signs were taped to the back of Danny's shirt. He was purposely tripped on his way to the pencil sharpener and then locked in the custodian's broom closet for an hour.

"Danny helped you with the multiplication tables," said Lizzie Tuttle to Jim. "Back off or you face me." Sandy Moore pushed Jim into the wall and asked, "What's your problem? Danny is a nice guy."

I didn't think he was nice. I laughed at the "Kick me" signs and suggested to Jim that he lock him in the girl's bathroom next time.

"We know all of that," said Joanna. "What about the 4th grade dance?"

"This is the worst part. I entered the school gymnasium before Danny. I had already eaten a cookie when I saw him enter the gym. He went straight into the boy's bathroom. I think he wanted to make sure his hair was still plastered with vaseline. There was no doubt about it in my mind.

"In the bathroom, he must have stepped on bubble gum and then on some toilet paper. At least that was how it looked when he returned to the gymnasium.

"Everyone in the gym knew that Danny had been in the bathroom. The toilet paper stuck to his shoe grew longer and longer with each step he took. Even Lizzie Tuttle and Sandy Moore pointed and whispered as he walked past. Jim Grow laughed out loud, but no one told Danny about the toilet paper as he circled the dance floor.

"I tried to hide behind Lucy McDougal when he walked past, but he saw me and stopped. Although I expected him to say, 'May I have this dance?' he did not. Instead he stammered, 'Gosh! You' re beautiful!'

"No one has ever said that to me before. And then it happened—the unthinkable. I asked Danny Lilly if he would like to dance with me," Susie said.

"No!" said Joanna and Wendy. "Not Danny Lilly."

"What's even worse is that I not only danced with Danny but also the toilet paper," said Susie. "Danny is a great dancer."

"Now for the big secret. Do you promise that you won't tell?" asked Susie.

Joanna and Wendy were too stunned to speak.

"I kissed Danny Lilly on the cheek when the dance ended," Susie exclaimed. "How can I ever go to school again? I have to run away from home—just the thought of me dancing with the school nerd and a streamer of toilet paper is nauseating. But I didn't just dance with him, I kissed him."

"You have to run away," said Wendy. "You may already be the joke of the school."

"This calls for drastic measures," said Joanna.

"I know," lamented Susie.

"We need a plan," said Joanna. "How about saying that you and I had a bet that you would never dance with Danny Lilly, and if you did dance with him and kiss him that I would give you a Milky Way and a free ticket to the Saturday matinee at the Crown Theater?"

"That might work," said Susie as she tried to wipe away her tears.

"Maybe that would work," said Wendy. "But how about this? Danny said that he would do your math homework for a year if you danced with him in the gym. He told you that if you kissed him on the cheek, he would also write your essays."

"That's good," said Susie.

Joanna said, "I'm not sure. Let's go for a walk so I can think."

As the three best friends walked toward Susie's house to consider the problem, they saw a little league game going on in the sandlot. Danny Lilly was up to bat.

"Let's watch him strike out," said Joanna.

Although Susie was hesitant, they walked toward the lot. Instead of striking out, they saw Danny slam the ball past right field and into the bushes. Everyone in the stands cheered, for his hit was the winning home run. The team congratulated Danny and the girls jumped off the stands yelling accolades as they ran toward the field.

Susie yelled, "Way to go, Danny!"

He heard her voice and turned around. "Susie, can I talk to you for a minute?" he shouted over the commotion.

"Sure," said Susie as she pushed her way through the crowd.

"About last night," said Danny, "I have thought a lot about it—the kiss and all. I hope that you will understand. I like Lizzie Tuttle now."

Susie watched as Danny picked up his glove and left the ball field with Lizzie. They were holding hands.

My Gift to You

"The Goodwill truck will be stopping by our house tomorrow to pick up unwanted furniture," my wife announced. "Are you ready to discard that wing back chair?"

Memories of yesteryear nearly overwhelmed me as I thought of that chair and what it meant to Tommy and me.

Knowing that cancer was winning the battle my father waged in 1970, Tommy and I sat in that chair next to his bed and read to him classic fairy tales and adventure stories. He delighted in the stories and said, "I'll miss these adventures. Be sure and find me in heaven so we can share them again." His favorite story was *Running Bear and the Drum.*

After the commotion created by the ambulance and tearful well-wishers subsided, Tommy and I sat in the chair and read Dad's favorite story hoping our father was still listening.

Once upon a time far away in an Indian village lived Chief Big Trout, a powerful man and a strong leader of his tribal nation. His name and fame were known from the land of tall trees to the cactus growing on the desert floor. Indians traversed the flatland to reach the top of the mountain just to speak with Big Trout and smoke a pipe with him.

Running Bear was very proud of his father, Big Trout, but feared that he could never follow in his footsteps. The problem was his name—Running Bear. He had called "Bear," before running to the teepee seeking safety in the arms of his mother. Braves reached for their bows and arrows only to discover the feared bear was a small raccoon scavenging in the village.

"Running Bear is the name of your son," the Medicine Man told Chief Big Trout. And Running Bear it had been ever since. It wasn't changed when he caught a large salmon in the river bed or when he lassoed the bucking stallion. His only hope of bidding farewell to the name Running Bear was at his eighth birthday celebration. At the celebration, the Medicine Man would give a new name to him to reflect the birthday present given by the chief.

Knowing of the new name, Running Bear looked up to the stars each night and wished for just the right gift from his father. He wished upon those stars so hard that he thought they might fall from the sky. But they didn't fall for he was the oldest son of Big Trout and even the stars knew him.

The fame of Big Trout was so great that Indians from near and far journeyed to the top of the mountain just to see the gift Running Bear would receive at the birthday celebration. Navajos came from Arizona, Piutes from Utah and Cheyenne from Wyoming. Each tribal member wore his festive headdress and feathers in honor of the exquisite gift that would soon be given.

That day—the day of celebration—hundreds of Indians crowded the mountain top, but all were silent. They waited for Big Trout to offer his gift to his son. The moment finally arrived. In a commanding voice Big Trout declared, "My son Running Bear is eight years old today." He then motioned for his son to stand next to him. Running Bear solemnly walked to his place beside the chief. His father then clapped his hands to summon a young brave. As the brave walked forward Big Trout said, "Go to my teepee and find the gift for my son with a feather atop."

The brave did the chief's bidding. He returned from the teepee carrying a drum with a feather atop.

"A drum," Running Bear said to himself. "There must be some mistake. A drum is the last birthday gift I want!"

Chief Big Trout didn't notice the tear in his son's eye. "I give you a drum. Keep this drum with you always, Running Bear," he said. "If you ever need me, just pound on the drum. As you pound, say these words: 'I want my father.'"

"Pounding Drum," shouted the Medicine Man. "Your new name is Pounding Drum." Although the group remained solemn during the pronunciation of the new name, Pounding Drum heard laughter as he took the drum and bowed to his father.

No one rushed forward to see his gift after the ceremony ended. It was easy for Pounding Drum to excuse himself from the dancing and chanting that followed. As he walked past the Navajos, Piutes and Cheyennes, it was as if they didn't notice him. It was the same as he walked past the teepees and out of the village.

He didn't stop to climb his favorite tree, watch the rushing river or gaze at the lizard on the valley floor. The deer in the meadow or the eagle flying overhead did not thwart his steps or catch his eyes. The only thing he looked at was that drum. Thoughts of the drum kept his feet moving and heart aching.

He climbed the next mountain and passed the briar patch and the fox lair. He quietly stepped beyond a curious cougar and bear cub but didn't slow his pace. It wasn't until he reached the top of the mountain that he screamed, "I hate my drum!" He picked up that drum and threw it as hard as he could down the mountainside. Pounding Drum was his new name—that was drum enough for him.

He stayed on that mountain top until dusk trying to figure out what happened to all those wishes upon the stars. Had the stars been laughing at him, too? And then there was the issue of Big Trout. The chief knew that he liked bows and arrows, tomahawks and ponies—not drums. Why did he give him a drum? The answer to his questions never came, even when the sun descended below the horizon. Although he didn't have answers, he was cold and hungry and wanted to return to the village.

Perhaps too quickly, he moved from the mountain top to what he had hoped was the valley below. But with every step he was moving farther from the valley and distancing himself from the village. He couldn't read the sky in the dark or see the familiar markings on the trees as he descended into the unknown wilderness. Therefore, he climbed to the top of the mountain again hoping for direction, but found his surroundings unfamiliar. He heard the cry of the wolf, the owl and the cougar.

"Where is my village? Where is my teepee? Where is Big Trout?" he shouted.

"Keep this drum with you always," Big Trout had said. "If you ever need me, just pound on the drum. As you pound, say these words: 'I want my father.'"

Pounding Drum scurried down the face of the mountain in search of the drum he had thrown away. He found it embedded at the base of a ponderosa pine. He cleaned off the loose gravel before beginning to pound.

"I want my father," he yelled with every pound. "I want my father."

Back in the Indian village so far away, Big Trout was holding a meeting with the chiefs of the gathered tribes who had come to celebrate the birthday. Just as Big Trout was passing the pipe from one tribal leader to another, he heard a very faint drum beating. He put down the pipe and said, "My son needs me."

With no other explanation, Big Trout left the tribal leaders to find his son. He ran from the village and passed his son's favorite tree, the rushing river and the valley floor. He didn't stop to look at the owl or other night predators, but he did stop again and again to listen for the drum beat.

He climbed the next mountain, past the briar patch and the fox lair, to reach the tree line. At the tree line, he heard the drum and a distant voice say, "I want my father." He quietly stepped beyond a curious cougar and mother bear with her cub.

Near the top of the mountain, he heard the intense beat of the drum and the strong words, "I want my father." It was then that Big Trout found his son.

"The drum and your words brought me to you," he said. "The dark sky nearly hid my path up the mountain, but the pounding of the drum and your voice kept me on course." He then lifted Pounding Drum on his shoulders before beginning his descent of the mountain.

"Shall I carry the drum for you?" he asked.

"No," his son said. "It's my birthday present. It brought you to me."

As Tommy and I finished reading the story of *Running Bear and the Drum*, I started to close the book, but Tommy stopped me. Pointing to an inscription on the last page he said, "Look! Dad wrote a note to you on this page. It must have been his way of giving you a birthday present."

I opened the book wide and read these words, "Steven, this is your eighth birthday. I wish that I could be with you and hear you read this book aloud. Like Big Trout in the story, I have written these words as my gift to you. And like Pounding Drum, just call out my name and I will come running to you. You may not see me, but I will always be there for you. I love you, Dad."

The years have come and gone since my eighth birthday. *Running Bear and the Drum* is still in my personal library. As for the wing back chair, it won't be going tomorrow with the Goodwill truck—too many memories to give away to someone that doesn't know the story.

Pipes in the Snow

Twenty years of family treasures, including remnants from my childhood, had been stored in the attic. Wanting to retrieve a few keepsakes before new owners took possession of the home, I ventured to the attic floor above.

"Clean up that mess while you're at it," said my wife. "When in doubt—throw it out."

"This is not going to be my best day," I told myself. But it was easy to part with unstrung tennis rackets and old football cleats. My first set of golf clubs and fishing pole were harder. But tossing old papers without reading them proved impossible. The teacher's note, "Brent is shy in class," brought a laugh as did my forged note, "Please excuse Brent for being absent yesterday. He wasn't feeling well, signed Mrs. Montgomery." But it was an essay, *Pipes in the Snow* written in junior high that stopped the cleaning process.

Pipes in the Snow
by Brent Montgomery

In 1973 my family moved to a cabin in the mountains of Colorado. Although it sounds like a great adventure for a mother and her two sons, the move was preceded by a divorce. Lacking means to live elsewhere, the summer cabin of my grandparents was my mother's only option. Boards put up to protect the cabin windows from harsh winter snow were removed as was the tattered flag that had once proudly flown on the pole outside as we tried to make the cabin our home. But nothing could be done to remove the isolation of living on a dirt road or the severity of the weather that was coming.

My mother chopped wood, hoping to ward off the winter blasts with a cozy fire. It seemed unnecessary as my brother and I played at the lake and fed peanuts to the squirrels in October. But within a month winter was upon us, and with it a heavy snow that buried cars and trucks and destroyed a nearby trailer park.

The severity of the weather led Colorado's governor to call out the national guard to transport people from the mountain to the valley below. "Soon military personnel will come to take us to safety," Mother said. But they never came. With telephone lines down, the only option was to stay on the mountain.

Instead of playing with my brother throughout the cabin as had been our custom in October, our play was confined to one room—the room with the fireplace. In that room our family played, ate and slept. For weeks we assumed that we were the only people on the mountain, especially after our radio lost power.

Then there was a knock on the door. Fearful of the unknown stranger who cast his shadow across our living room, Mother cautiously looked out the window. "It's a man from church," she said as she recognized Ken Stoddard, a veteran of the Korean War.

The door was opened and after removing his snow shoes, Mr. Stoddard walked inside. "Just walking around the mountain checking on who is still up here," he explained. "I have found the Jones, Petersons and McCalls safe. How are you doing? Do you need anything?" he asked.

"Thanks for checking on us. We are fine. We thought that we were the only ones on the mountain," said Mother. "Glad to know that we have friends. Come warm yourself by the fire. Would you like Brent to throw another log on the fire?"

Mr. Stoddard laughed at the suggestion and said, "If your son Brent can tough it out so can I!" Then he asked, "What's wrong with your furnace?"

"Nothing's wrong," said Mother. "We don't have one."

The conversation turned to other subjects like the Anderson's caved-in trailer and ice on the main road, but before Mr. Stoddard left he asked, "Brent can you show me the other rooms in the cabin?"

"Button up," I said. "It is really cold." I took Mr. Stoddard through the old cabin and showed him my secret hideouts. I then bid him farewell as he put on his snowshoes and left in hopes of finding other families still living on the mountain.

I later learned that at each home where families were found, Mr. Stoddard spoke of us not having a modern heating system.

"That's crazy," said Ned Thurston.

"No one would live up here this winter without heat," remarked Pete Evans.

Randy Porter exclaimed, "Impossible!"

Two days later I looked out the window and saw pipes walking through the snow. "Mom, there are pipes walking through the snow," I said. I pulled her to the window and pointed outside. She saw small and large pipes being carried by men and young teenagers that we had seen at church, the post office and the grocery store. Leading the procession was Ken Stoddard.

From selecting assorted parts to crawling where only spiders had ventured before, Mr. Stoddard made sure that the heating system was installed "first rate" in our cabin. He watched as the flooring was cut and the pipes carefully hung. His meticulous supervision delayed the project again and again, although he knew that no money would be exchanged.

"Will it work?" I asked him as we huddled around the fireplace.

"Keep your finger's crossed," he said.

I did until I heard the soft roar of the engine and felt the warmth of the heat.

"How can I repay you?" Mother asked.

"Just raise a flag for me," he said jokingly.

His attempt to be funny was not taken in jest by my family. Our first purchase after the snow melted was an American flag. My brother and I worked for hours to shine the flagpole until it glistened.

Mother telephoned Mr. Stoddard and asked, "Can you stop by our cabin after work?"

"Sure," said Ken.

When he arrived, we were standing by the flagpole waiting to greet him. Mother reminded him of the heating system and his comment, "Just raise a flag for me." My brother and I then carefully unfolded our new American flag before hoisting it in the air. We all sang, "The Star Spangled Banner." As Mr. Stoddard wiped a tear from his cheek, I said "You're the kind of man I want to be."

My wife's voice pulled me back into the attic: "Are you alright? I'm not hearing any movement up there."

"Yes, dear," I replied as I reached for the next essay.

53 Pennies & A Comic Book

No one ever anticipated that Karl Ward would be racing on Ocean Boulevard for a chance to deliver milk door-to-door, but then again no one had known how widespread the Great Depression would be. Karl, a graduate of George Washington Law School, had been top in his class. "You are the hope of America, the promise of tomorrow," the law school president had whispered to him at the graduation exercise.

But that day on Ocean Boulevard no one was whispering to him or anyone else about hope or the future of America. The crowd looked over the three hundred contestants and wondered aloud who would win the chance to deliver milk door-to-door—in other words, a chance to leave the bread lines and earn a wage.

Karl wanted to win that race. His silver medals from track meets at the University of Texas weren't that tarnished yet. "On your mark, get set, go!" yelled the announcer at the starting line. Karl ran like the wind, and like the wind he was first over the finish line. The crowd roared in appreciation, but it was the manager of the Weber Creamery who offered Karl a job that brought tears of gratitude to the recent law school graduate. Well-wishers moved close to slap him on the back, but the envious turned away to face the bread lines once again.

There was no doubt that Karl's prospect for the future was better after the race, although his dream of a Nash, a round of golf and vacationing on the French Riviera would wait. Employment as a milk man enabled him to meet the necessary expenses of his growing family but not the extras. Christmas gifts and roller coaster rides at the Long Beach Pike would have to wait another season.

But wanting the impossible for Christmas 1937, Karl saved pennies from his wage to buy a gift for each family member—a scarf for grandma, a pendant for his wife and licorice sticks for his sons. By December 20, 1937 he had saved two dollars in pennies—enough to buy the modest gifts. He exchanged the pennies for a crisp two dollar bill at the corner bank before running three blocks to the fancy department store.

He stopped to gaze in the department store window to view the shiny red bike, the blue scooter and a stuffed teddy bear before entering. "These would make great gifts," he thought, "but not this year." This was the Depression.

Karl noticed that he was not alone at the storefront window. "I suppose you are wishing for the bike?" he said to the small boy also looking longingly in the display window.

"No! I was wishing for that coat hanging in the corner," the boy said.

Seeing the coat for the first time Karl said, "That's a woman's coat, son."

"I know," said the boy. "I wish that I had the money to buy it for my mother, but I don't. It's the Depression, sir. Only rich folks like you have coats."

"Rich? Me?" Karl thought to himself as he stared at the young boy wrapped in a blanket to keep warm. Pulling the two dollar bill from his pocket Karl handed it to the boy, saying, "Now you are rich like me. I think your mother will like that coat."

The boy smiled and ran inside the store and put the crisp two-dollar bill down on the counter. Karl watched as the storekeeper took the woman's coat from the display window, wrapped it in a box and tied it with a bright red ribbon. It was a happy, memorable scene, but as Karl walked toward his home his pace slowed. The realization that charity to a stranger had compromised his own family's Christmas weighed heavily upon him.

At home, he felt obliged to explain his impulsive kindness to his sons. Reluctantly, he told them of saving pennies and of his hasty gift to the young stranger. "I am sorry," Karl said. "There will not be Christmas in our home this year."

"Don't worry, Santa Claus will bring us a gift," Davey said.

"No, he won't," Karl replied. "Santa Claus is also having a bad year."

"Santa's sleigh is filled with toys," countered Davey.

It was Ryan who knew the consequences of his Dad's charitable act. "Don't worry about presents. It doesn't matter," he said.

In spite of his consoling words, Karl knew it would matter on Christmas Day. The next day at work he was filled with self-pity.

"What's wrong, Karl?" other delivery men asked him.

His trite reply, "Nothing," was unconvincing. Jokes, cheerful banter and a company Christmas party did not change his mood. Not even a kiss from his wife and hugs from his sons as he returned home could brighten his spirits.

It wasn't until he entered the kitchen and saw pennies on his dinner plate that his mood changed. "What is this?" he asked as he counted fifty-three pennies. "Who did this?"

To answer his own question, he hurried next door to see his friend Howard. "Did you put pennies on my dinner plate?" Karl asked.

"Pennies on a dinner plate? What are you talking about?" Howard replied. "If you find out who's serving money for dinner, tell them to send some my way."

Returning to his kitchen Karl found Davey and Ryan laughing. "Dad, the pennies are from us. Now you can buy Christmas presents," said Ryan. "We collected old soda pop bottles from the neighbors. Mr. Riley gave us a penny for each bottle."

"Mrs. Wilson gave us a penny for washing her windows and Mr. Evans, two pennies for running errands," exclaimed Davey.

"Don't forget Mr. Blackman," said Ryan. "He gave three pennies for cleaning his garage. We got most of our pennies from selling our old comic books. Who needs Superman anyway?"

Ryan and Davey expected Dad to laugh, but he didn't. "You love those comic books. I've seen you reading them over and over again in the field," said Karl. He then started to cry.

"What's wrong?" Ryan asked.

"Nothing's wrong, everything is right!" Karl said as he wiped away his tears. "Christmas will be wonderful. Your gift to me is more than generous."

Christmas 1937 was wonderful for Karl's family. Grandma loved her scarf, mother her shiny pendant and Ryan and Davey the licorice sticks.

As the years passed the family never forgot Christmas 1937. Each year before his death, Karl went to a department store on December 20th seeking a young boy who needed a gift. When he returned home he would discover anew that his sons had placed fifty-three cents on his dinner plate. Karl would hand each son a licorice stick and an old edition of a Superman comic book. He would then tell the story of the race down Ocean Boulevard, his job as a milkman, the little boy at the department store and the fifty-three pennies, as if it had been the best time of his life.

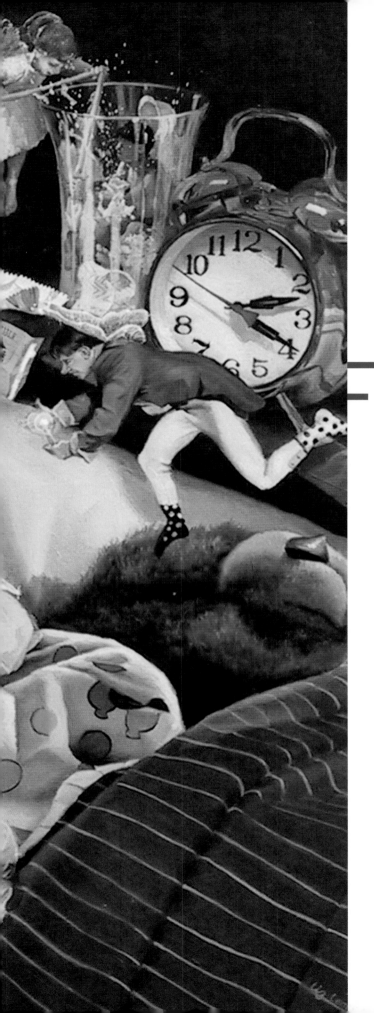

Hair Fairies

The move to Washington, D.C. has taken its toll on our family. My husband is often gone on government assignments, leaving me to make many decisions alone. I have no problem with normal decisions like shopping or paying bills, but lately I have become very worried about our son Kevin. I took him to see a child psychologist who said, "He should have grown out of his fantasies by now." Unfortunately, he hasn't.

Every morning he talks about "hair fairies." That's right—hair fairies. It doesn't appear that his fairies resemble Cinderella's godmother or a tooth fairy. According to Kevin they are small creatures who spend the night hours pulling his hair to create the unkempt look he awakens to in the morning. I have tried to assure him that he has cowlicks and not hair fairies that cause his morning look, but he counters by asking, "Can cowlicks cause me to dream? Hair fairies do." His dreams made no sense until this morning. That was the reason for our emergency visit to the psychologist.

"I went into his room as usual and found that his hair was askew—actually, it looked spiked," I told the psychologist.

"Wake up, sleepyhead," I said. "It's time to start the day."

"I had another dream last night," said Kevin. "This time it was about Spencer."

Although I had grown weary of his fantasy world I dutifully said, "Tell me about it while you get dressed."

"Is today Spencer's first day at school?" Kevin asked.

"It sure is," I said. "He left about twenty minutes ago. He was so excited. His friend Ross was meeting him at the street corner. I think this will be Spencer's best school year yet."

"Not at first," Kevin said. "In my dream Spencer gave you a hug and then headed off to school. His friend Ross was not waiting for him at the corner like he promised. Spencer waited for Ross for several minutes but then hurried on so that he would not be late. As he was running toward school, Butch LeFevre purposely tripped him.

"'Where are you going so fast?' Butch asked.

"'To school,' said Spencer, as he stood up and brushed off his pant legs.

"'No you're not,' said Butch. 'Not unless you can get past me!' Then for no reason at all he punched Spencer in the face."

"That's ridiculous Kevin," I said. "Let's get you dressed and go downstairs to eat breakfast."

"I'm not through telling you about Spencer," Kevin said. "In the next part of the dream I saw him running home with his hand covering his nose. He was crying. He entered the house and yelled, 'I'm never going to school again. I hate Washington, D.C. Why did Dad have to move anyway?'

"You hurried to the front door and saw blood on his hand. You knelt down to get a good look at him and asked what had happened. You were angry after he told you about

Butch and insisted that he write a note to him: *'I want to fight you in two months on October 5th in the school yard at two o'clock. Until that time, don't bother me. — Signed, Spencer Post.'*

"You then walked Spencer to school and made sure he handed the note to Butch. Butch laughed out loud after reading it but upon seeing the anger in your eyes, he figured he'd better do it.

"On the way home from the elementary school you stopped at the library and checked out books on the art of self-defense. You and Spencer read the books together. Meanwhile classmates learned about the note and talked non-stop about October 5th, wondering aloud whether Spencer could fight, let alone survive the ordeal. A few students even told their teachers. Teachers told the principal, and the principal telephoned you.

"'Mrs. Post are you sure you want Spencer to fight Butch?' the principal asked.

"'Yes,' you assured him and asked him to dismiss classes at two in the afternoon of October the 5th so that all could see the fight."

"Kevin, I wouldn't say that to a principal," I told him. "Hurry and finish getting dressed. It's time for breakfast."

"More stuff happened in the dream. Let me finish," said Kevin.

Seeing that I had grown quiet, he continued. "After a week of reading defense books Spencer said, 'I need more than a book to help me fight Butch LeFevre.'

"You agreed and bought a punching bag and then set it up in our garage. Spencer was frustrated with the punching bag until our neighbor Mr. Richardson saw him.

"'Do you want to be a boxer?' he asked.

"'No,' said Spencer. 'I just want to defend myself against Butch LeFevre on October 5th. We're going to fight and the whole school knows it. The principal is dismissing classes so everyone can watch.'

"'Is Butch bothering you, too?' asked Mr. Richardson. 'He's also causing problems for my son Sammy. Maybe I can help. I used to be an amateur boxer when I was younger.'

"Mr. Richardson was a great boxer. He could beat Mohammed Ali. But Mr. Richardson wasn't going to fight Butch. Spencer was and the outcome seemed unsure.

"'I have a fever and can't go to school,' Spencer announced on October 5th. Funny, his temperature was normal. 'I have a stomach ache,' said Spencer.

"'You're fine and will win the fight,' you told him.

"'How do you know?' Spencer asked.

"'I just do,' you said.

"That morning at school no one could concentrate—not the students, teachers or principal and especially not Spencer. Everyone was talking about the fight and wondering how bad Spencer would be hurt before the principal stepped in to rescue him.

"The school bell rang at five minutes before two that afternoon. 'School is dismissed to the playground,' the principal said over the loud speaker. The students ran to the playground and formed a large circle. Spencer and Butch stepped into the middle of the circle.

"'If you want to live, you had better run,' Butch yelled.

"Spencer didn't run. He walked right up to Butch and punched him in the nose. It took just one punch and Butch fell to the ground. Friends rushed to congratulate Spencer. Even Butch shook his hand.

"But Spencer wasn't thinking about Butch. He ran home to tell you. He burst in the front door yelling, 'Mom, I won.'"

"Kevin," I said, "Spencer is having a great day at school. Those hair fairies of yours are mistaken. These dreams have to stop!"

Just then the front door opened. Spencer entered the house and yelled, "I am never going to school again. I hate Washington, D.C. Why did Dad have to move anyway?"

"I hurried to the front door and saw blood on his hand. That's why I'm at the emergency clinic today," I told the psychologist. "Is there such a thing as a hair fairy?"

Field Day with Alfred Ledbottom

My dad owned a small peach orchard and my mother worked in a packing house in Musella, Georgia. Picking peaches or packing peaches was the unfinished dinner conversation at our house until I entered third grade and Alfred Ledbottom, a skinny version of Icabod Crane, became my teacher. After that peaches took a back seat to Mr. Ledbottom's daily mishaps. If he didn't have bad luck, he wouldn't have had any luck at all.

Daily he entered the classroom disheveled in appearance and muttering excuses as to why he was late. His arms were always filled with books, papers or a science project that invariably had gone bad. Although everyday could be considered memorable, nothing came close to one field day with Alfred Ledbottom.

"Class, in an hour we will be leaving for our field day excursion to complete our unit on nature, and to release our butterflies into the wild. There are a few things you need to know before we get on the bus. In the fields you will see many spiders," he said. "Come close so that all can see. Don't be afraid, Elizabeth, spiders are our friends."

As the class sat in a circle on the floor, they watched as Mr. Ledbottom allowed an eight-legged spider to crawl out of a glass jar. He spoke of its color, its legs and then reiterated that "spiders are our friends."

"Are there any questions about the spiders that we will see on our field trip today?" he asked. Hearing none he purposefully stepped on the spider before moving to his next topic—a wasps' nest. It was hard for the rest of us to change subjects so quickly, as we watched the spider's twitching legs. We sat there in disbelief, witnessing our newfound friend's slow demise.

"Avoid such objects on our field day excursion," Mr. Ledbottom continued, holding the wasps' nest for all to see. When classmates expressed fear he assured them, "There are no wasps in this nest." To prove his point he put his finger in a small opening. As angry wasps flew from the opening, some students ran from the classroom screaming, but I stayed to watch. I knew my family would want to hear about the wasps at dinner.

Mr. Ledbottom fought them off valiantly until two or three of those critters flew down his shirt collar. Suddenly he tore off his coat and shirt. He slapped himself again and again before doing his version of "stop, drop and roll."

"Help me!" he yelled.

Tommy threw a large eraser at him. Bobby leaped forward and hit him with a textbook in the ribs several times. Following Bobby's lead, I kicked him again and again in the back. Whether it was the eraser, the textbook or my kicks the wasps stopped stinging him.

Mr. Ledbottom stood up, put on his shirt and tried to compose himself. He then went to the door to tell the screaming children in the hall that it was safe to return. But just then the principal, Mrs. Pitt, an ample woman whom I called "Peach Pit", came running into the classroom determined to know the cause of the commotion.

"What is the problem?" she yelled.

"Wasps **stung** Mr. Ledbottom," said Emily Parsons.

"Wasps **are stinging** Mr. Ledbottom?!" the principal shrieked in alarm!

Before anyone could correct her, she grabbed our teacher around the waist, lifted him in the air, threw him to the floor and sat on him in hopes of destroying the wasps. Mr. Ledbottom flailed his hands and in a barely audible voice whispered, "Get off! I can't breathe!" I couldn't help but think of his resemblance to the spider.

Before the comparison to our eight-legged friend was complete, Tommy and I rushed to pull the principal off Mr. Ledbottom. Although we had hoped that she would rise gracefully, it took eight classmates pulling and singing "Tote that barge, lift that bale" to lift her. She left the classroom in a huff. When we could no longer hear her footsteps in the hall, Mr. Ledbottom expressed profound gratitude and assured us that we had saved his life.

Now it was time for the final phase of his lesson—safety on the school bus. As he took assorted marbles and tacks from a sack he asked, "What happens if any of these are found on the floor of the bus?"

Debbie said, "Someone might step on a tack and get hurt."

"You might fall down," said Emily.

"You're both right," said Mr. Ledbottom. "I am going to demonstrate the possible hazards of these objects by attempting to walk on them." It wasn't the first marble that propelled him to the floor, but the second one got him. To recapture his balance he put out his hands to soften the blow. That was when he discovered the tacks.

After rising to his feet and pulling out each tack one-by-one, he pushed forward with the safety lesson. Walking toward a classroom window he said, "Never put your head out the window on a moving bus." After putting his own head out the window he asked Bobby about possible consequences. Rather than speak of the danger associated with such a reckless action, Bobby stepped to the window and pulled the top window down. I don't think Bobby had imagined that it would come down with such vengeance.

I would have gotten Mr. Ledbottom an ace bandage for his neck if I hadn't heard Peach Pit's voice over the loud speaker: "Mr. Ledbottom bring your class to the bus now. It's time for us to go!"

The bus ride proved uneventful and it appeared that the mishaps of Alfred Ledbottom were over, but actually the biggest was yet to come. Near the end of our excursion, Mr. Ledbottom announced: "Class, it is now time for the great event we have all been waiting for — the release of our monarch butterflies. Let's all count to three and then open our jars." We watched as our butterflies emerged from their captivity.

Suddenly, the unthinkable occurred. A butterfly flew into the mouth of the principal. Mrs. Pitt gasped for air and those watching thought she had swallowed a monarch. Although she claimed that the butterfly flew out of her mouth, Mr. Ledbottom wasn't sure. He gave her mouth-to-mouth resuscitation until the principal doubled her fist and smashed him with a right uppercut. It knocked him out cold.

It wasn't until the principal was safely seated next to the bus driver that Tommy was given permission to wake up Mr. Ledbottom and get him on the bus. With both of them in their seats, the driver announced, "All children are to get on the bus, take a seat and not say a word."

Needless to say the bus ride back to school was awkward. We didn't know what was going to happen to our teacher. Tommy whispered, "I think Peach Pit will fire him."

After the bus stopped at school Mr. Ledbottom got off first. "Thank you for a lovely day Mrs. Pitt," he said as he held out his hand to steady the principal as she stepped from the bus. She refused his gesture and said, "Don't ever touch me again!"

Waiting to greet them in front of the school was the district superintendent. "I am so happy to see you both together. I have great news! The school board has just unanimously voted to offer the position of vice-principal to Mr. Ledbottom. Congratulations, Alfred!"

Mr. Ledbottom turned to Mrs. Pitt and gave her a hug before going merrily on his way.

Taking a deep breath, Mrs. Pitt clenched her teeth and muttered, "School dismissed." She walked toward her office with a slight twitch in her leg.